Tom and Ricky
and the
Roving Robot Mystery

Bob Wright

High Noon Books
Novato, California

Cover Design: Nancy Peach
Interior Illustrations: Herb Heidinger
Story: Miriam Ylvusaker and Deena Aerenson

Glossary: robbery, computer, unlock, secrets

International Standard Book Number: 0-87879-398-4

10 09 08 07 06 05 04
15 14 13 12 11 10 09 08 (

You'll enjoy all the High Noon Books.
Write for a free full list of titles.

CONTENTS

CHAPTER 1

At the Computer Fair

Tom and Ricky stopped their bikes. They were in front of Eddie's house.

"Where is he?" Tom asked.

"He said he would be waiting for us," Ricky said.

"Eddie! Eddie!" Tom called out.

Eddie came to the door.

"Come on. Let's get going. It's time to go to the Computer Fair," Tom said.

"I forgot all about it," Eddie said.

"We better hurry. There will be a lot of people there," Ricky said.

"Wait. I need to get my book bag," Eddie said.

"Your book bag?" Ricky asked.

"I have to take it. It has my computer games in it," Eddie said.

"Why are you going to take them to the fair?" Tom asked.

"They are going to let people play their own games," Eddie answered.

"Is Patches coming with us?" Tom asked.

"I think we can take him," Ricky answered.

The three boys got on their bikes. They went down Front Street. They could see lots of people at the Computer Fair.

They parked their bikes and locked them. Then they went in. Patches went in with them.

"Look at all the people," Tom said.

"Look at all the games," Eddie said.

"There are war games and mystery games," Tom said.

"Look! There's a robot!" Ricky said.

"Do you think it will move around here?" Tom asked.

"Maybe it will," Ricky said.

"Come on over here. Let's play a mystery game," Eddie said.

Tom and Ricky went over to Eddie.

"What mystery game do you want to play?" Tom asked.

"Mine. I brought one of my own," Eddie said.

"What's it like?" Tom asked.

"The computer gives you clues to a robbery. You tell the computer who took the money. I'll show you," Eddie said.

Eddie pushed the stick. A little man moved up and down. Then he moved left and right.

Eddie said, "The little man will look for clues. Tom, you try it."

"That little man looks like the robot we saw," Tom said. He pushed the stick. The little man went into a room. He found a red box. The red box was a clue.

Then Tom said, "It's your turn, Ricky."

4

Ricky pushed the stick. "Look at that. The little man is moving faster."

"That is good. It tells you the clue is a good one," Eddie said.

Then Ricky said, "OK, Eddie. Now it's your turn."

Eddie pushed the stick. The little man went off the screen.

"Why did the man go off the screen?" Tom asked.

"Look. I'll bring him back." Eddie pushed the stick again. The little man came back on the screen. This time the man had a blue box.

"Whose turn is it now?" Ricky asked.

Patches began to bark. Tom laughed.

5

"Maybe Patches thinks it is his turn," Tom said.

Patches didn't stop barking.

"What's going on? He must see something," Ricky said.

Patches moved in back of the boys. He kept right on barking.

The boys looked at Patches. Then they looked up.

"Will you look at that," Eddie said.

"It's that robot. It's coming right over to us," Eddie said.

"And it's carrying a book bag," Eddie said.

CHAPTER 2

A Talking Robot

The three boys looked at the robot. It walked over to them.

"The robot walks just like we do," Eddie said.

"He can move his arms and his head, too," Ricky said.

The robot looked at the boys. Then it said, "Hello. My name is Robert. I am a robot."

"He can even talk. He sounds like us," Eddie said.

"You answer him, Eddie," Ricky said.

"Look, I think the robot is going to talk again," Tom said.

"Hello. My name is Robert. I am a robot."

"What are your names?" the robot asked.

"You talk to him, Eddie. Tell him your name," Tom said.

"My name is Eddie and these are my friends. This is Ricky's dog. His name is Patches," Eddie said.

The robot moved closer to the boys. He was very large.

"Look, Eddie. The robot has a book bag like yours," Ricky said.

"What do you think he has in it?" Eddie asked.

There were many people at the fair. Some people were playing computer games. Some people were watching the robot and the boys.

"What is in your book bag, Eddie?" the robot asked.

"My computer games," Eddie answered.

The robot moved closer to the boys. Patches started to bark. The boys moved away from the robot.

"Let's start playing our mystery game again," Tom said.

"Whose turn was it last?" Tom asked.

"I don't know. Do you know whose turn it was, Ricky?" Eddie said.

"No, I don't. Why don't we begin over again?" Ricky said.

"Good. Let's start playing," Eddie said.

The boys began playing their mystery game.

Then a man walked over to them.

"Hello, boys," the man said. It was Mr. West.

"Hello, Mr. West. I see you are not at your video store today," Ricky said.

"No, I came to the Computer Fair because I wanted to see the new games," Mr. West said.

"There is a robot at the fair," Eddie said.

"Yes, I saw him talking to you," Mr. West said.

"He asked us our names," Tom said.

"Did you answer him?" Mr. West asked.

"We told him our names," Eddie said.

"And the robot told us his name is Robert," Tom said.

"He has a book bag just like Eddie's," Ricky said.

"Mr. West, how can robots talk?" Tom asked.

"Robots cannot talk by themselves," Mr. West said.

"Can they walk by themselves?" Tom asked.

"No, they cannot walk or talk on their own. They need a man to tell them what to do," Mr. West said.

Just then Patches began to bark. Patches was looking at the people.

"Why is he barking?" Mr. West asked.

"I think he is barking at that man," Eddie said.

"What man?" Mr. West asked.

Eddie pointed to a short man standing back a little way.

"He is watching the robot. I think he is also watching us," Ricky said.

"I see the box, too. He uses the box to make the robot walk and talk. The robot cannot do anything alone. He needs the man to help him," Mr. West said.

CHAPTER 3

Meeting Mr. Roberts

The boys kept on watching the robot. Then the man with the box came over.

"Hello," Mr. West said.

"Hello. I see that you like my robot," the man said.

"Can you tell us about him?" Mr. West asked.

"Why do you want to know?" the man said.

"I own the video store in this town. I like to know about things like this," Mr. West said.

"I see. Let me tell you. My name is Mr. Roberts. That's how I named the robot Robert. I made him myself," Mr. Roberts said.

"I think you have done a fine job," Mr. West said.

"Thank you. The people at the Computer Fair let me bring him. Robert walks around and talks to people. He's the only robot at the Fair," Mr. Roberts said.

"That's right. I read about him. He's Robert, the Roving Robot," Ricky said.

"Yes. I keep him moving around," Mr. Roberts said.

"Why did you put a book bag on him?" Eddie asked.

"I thought it would look good on him," Mr. Roberts answered.

"I have one just like it," Eddie said.

"Why did you put a book bag on him?" Eddie asked.

"Eddie used his to bring some of his games here," Tom said.

"What's in Robert's book bag?" Eddie asked.

"I put books in it. The kids like to see Robert carrying books," Mr. Roberts said.

"I must go now. Robert has to keep moving around the Fair," Mr. Roberts said.

"Maybe we'll see you again," Tom called out.

"Well, boys. I have to get back to my video store. Drop in when you can," Mr. West said. Then he left.

"What do you want to do now?" Tom asked.

"We could go back and play Eddie's game again," Ricky said.

"Let's walk around. We can see more things here at the Fair," Eddie said.

"That's a good idea. We can play your game later, Eddie," Ricky said.

The three boys walked around the fair. They looked at all the new things.

"Look. There's Robert again. He's talking to some other people," Ricky said. The boys turned around to watch Robert the Robot.

"He doesn't have his book bag," Eddie said.

"Maybe he got tired carrying it around," Ricky said.

"Very funny," Eddie said.

"Let's go back and play your game, Eddie," Tom said.

"That's a good idea. We don't have much more time. The Fair will be closing soon," Eddie said.

CHAPTER 4

One More Game

The boys walked back to play one more game. There wasn't much time left. The Fair was going to be closing very soon.

"Eddie. Let's try another one of your games," Tom said.

"OK. I'll get my book bag. We can try another one," Eddie said.

Tom and Ricky went back to the computer they had been using.

"I haven't seen Patches," Ricky said.

"I forgot all about him, too," Tom said.

"Patches! Patches!" Ricky called out.

"We'll never find him. There are too many people walking around. Maybe he's hiding somewhere," Tom said.

All of a sudden Eddie came back. "I can't find it. I can't find my book bag," he said.

"We're looking for Patches. We can't find him," Ricky said.

Just then, Robert went by. "Hello, Eddie. Hello, Tom. Hello, Ricky," the robot said.

"Robert, have you seen my book bag? I see you have yours. I can't find mine," Eddie said.

"Sure I know where your book bag is. It's over there with Ricky's dog," Robert said.

The boys looked all around. Then Ricky said, "There it is. It's under that big computer. Patches is sitting on it."

"It's under that big computer.
Patches is sitting on it."

"How did it get there?" Eddie asked.

"Maybe Patches dragged it there," Tom said.

Eddie walked over to get his book bag. He picked it up. "Is this my book bag? It seems bigger than mine," he said.

"It looks like your book bag. It must be yours," Tom said.

The Computer Fair was ending. People were going home. The boys went outside to their bikes. They unlocked them. Then they rode down Front Street. Patches was in back of them.

"That was a good fair," Eddie said.

"It was fun. I never saw a robot before," Tom said.

"I didn't know robots could walk like that. They sure can do a lot of things," Ricky said.

"All you need is that box to make them work," Eddie said.

"What's in the box?" Tom asked.

"It has computer parts in it. The man uses the box to start and stop the robot," Eddie said.

"How does the robot talk?" Ricky asked.

"The man uses the box for that, too. The box is what makes the robot talk," Eddie said.

"Can the man make the robot do anything he wants it to do?" Tom asked.

"The man can make the robot do many things. But the robot can't do everything people can," Eddie said.

The boys were almost home. Patches began to bark again. They looked behind them. They saw the man with the robot behind him.

"Look, do you see what I see? There's that man with the robot," Ricky said.

"I see them, too. What's going on? Where are they going?" Eddie asked.

"I don't know. Do you think maybe they might live near here?" Tom asked.

"I never saw them before today. Where did they come from?" Eddie asked.

"Where could they be going?" Tom asked.

"Do you think they are going where we are going? Let's get back to my house. I want to tell my mom and dad what's going on," Ricky said.

CHAPTER 5

The Mystery in the Book Bag

When the boys got to Ricky's house they locked their bikes and went inside. Ricky's mom was there.

"Hi, Mom," Ricky said.

"Hi, Ricky. Hello, boys. Did you have a good time at the Computer Fair?" Ricky's mom asked.

"It was fun," Tom said.

"We played a space game on the computer. Mr. West was there, too," Eddie said.

"And, Dad, we saw a robot. And we saw a man with a box telling the robot what to do," Ricky said.

"They must live on this street. We saw them coming this way," Tom said.

"I don't think they do. I've never seen them before," Ricky's dad said.

"Maybe they want my computer games. I think I'll just make sure they're all here," Eddie said.

Eddie went over to the table and picked up his book bag.

"Something is funny about this book bag," Eddie said.

"Let's open it up," Tom said.

Eddie opened the top of the book bag to look inside. Ricky and Tom watched him.

"Look at this! These aren't my things," Eddie said.

"You're right, Eddie. This isn't your bag," Tom said.

"Where are all your computer games?" Ricky asked.

"I don't know. Look at this big box. This is why my book bag was so hard to carry," Eddie said.

"Where did that box come from?" Ricky's dad asked.

"It must be from the Computer Fair," Eddie said.

"What could be in there?" Ricky's mom asked.

"Let's take a look," Ricky's dad said.

"Let's take a look," Ricky's dad said.

29

Eddie took the box out of the book bag. He put it on the table. It was black and had a blue lock on it.

"Is it unlocked? Let's see if we can get it open," Ricky said.

The boys tried to pull the lock open.

"It's got to be locked," Ricky said.

"I don't think we can get it open," Eddie said.

"Why don't we look for something to help us get it open?" Tom said.

"Wait, boys. We don't know what's in the box. We don't know where it came from. It might have things in it that are not ours," Ricky's dad said.

"I really would like to know what's in there. What if it's money?" Eddie said.

"Maybe there are computer games in it," Tom said.

"Or maybe there are secrets about robots. I wish we could look and find out," Ricky said.

"Let's wait, boys. I think we should call Sergeant Collins. We want him here when we open it," Ricky's mom said.

"That's a good idea. I am sure Sergeant Collins could come over right away," Ricky's dad said.

Ricky's mother went to the phone to call Sergeant Collins. The boys sat around the table waiting. Just then the door bell rang.

"I'll get it," Ricky's dad said.

Ricky's dad opened the door. The boys could hear him talking to someone.

"No, you cannot come in. What do you want?" Ricky's dad asked.

Ricky went over to the door. Eddie and Tom came over, too. They saw the man with the robot. The man looked at Eddie.

"This is the boy who took our book bag. We want it back," the man said.

"Is this your book bag or is it Eddie's? We are not sure. Sergeant Collins will be here soon. Why don't you and your robot come in and wait for him? Then we will find out what's going on here," Ricky's dad said.

CHAPTER 6

A Computer Robber

The man at the door said, "No, we do not want to come in. That is our book bag. We want you to give it to us now. If you won't give it to us, we will find someone who will make you give it back."

The boys moved away from the door. They were not sure what the man would do.

Ricky's dad said, "I won't give you this book bag. You can wait here for Sergeant Collins or you can leave now."

"All right, we will see about all this," the man said. Then he and the robot turned around and walked away very fast.

"If you won't give it to us, we will find someone who will make you give it back."

"I hope Sergeant Collins gets here soon," Ricky's mom said.

Ricky's mom and dad and the boys sat down.

"What could be in the box?" Eddie asked.

"It must be something secret. The man was mad when we would not give it to him," Ricky said.

The doorbell rang. Ricky's dad went to answer it.

"Hello, Sergeant Collins. Am I glad to see you!" Ricky's dad said.

"What's going on?" Sergeant Collins asked.

"The boys can tell you more about it than I can," Ricky's dad said.

The boys talked fast. They told Sergeant Collins about the man and the robot.

"The man said the book bag here is his. I know it is not my book bag because my computer games are gone, and this big box is not mine," Eddie said.

"Let's take a look at the box," Sergeant Collins said.

Sergeant Collins took a look at the lock.

"We need a way to open this box. I might have something with me," Sergeant Collins said.

Sergeant Collins pulled a lot of keys from his coat.

"One of these might work," Sergeant Collins said.

Sergeant Collins tried one of the small keys in the lock. It didn't work. Then he tried another key. The lock still did not open.

"Let's try one more time," Sergeant Collins said.

This time Sergeant Collins opened the lock. The boys stood close to him so they could see inside the black box. It was full of papers.

"What are all these papers?" Tom asked.

"They have numbers and lines on them," Ricky said.

"I think I know what they are. I have heard about this man. He takes people's plans for making robots. Then he sells the plans," Sergeant Collins said.

"But why did he want my book bag? And why did he give me his?" Eddie asked.

"I told the Computer Fair people about this man. He knew the Computer Fair people would look in the robot's bag," the Sergeant said.

"That's why they did it! That way I would carry the plans out of the Fair for the man," Eddie said.

"Do you think he will come back, Sergeant Collins?" Tom asked.

"Yes, I think he will. Boys, you are going to have to help me," Sergeant Collins said.

"How will we do that?" Eddie asked.

CHAPTER 7

The Robot Gets A New Home

The boys looked at Sergeant Collins. They wanted to hear his plan.

"Eddie, I want you to ask him what is in the black box. Ricky, I want you to ask him to show you what is in the box. I will lock it up again now," Sergeant Collins said.

"We will ask the man some questions. Then we will take the man and the robot down to Mr. West's video store. We will let Mr. West look at the plans," Sergeant Collins said.

"Mr. West will be able to tell us more about the plans," Eddie said.

"And then we will know the answer to our mystery," Ricky said.

"I hear the doorbell. That must be the man. Don't forget our plan, boys," Sergeant Collins said.

Sergeant Collins opened the door. The man and the robot stood there. The man looked mad.

"I am here to get my book bag," the man said.

"We are not sure we can give it back to you," Sergeant Collins said.

"What's in that black box?" Eddie asked.

"The plans for my robot," the man said.

"Will you unlock the box for us? We would like to see those plans," Tom said.

The man took keys from his pocket. He unlocked the lock and opened the box.

"See, I told you it was just plans," the man said.

The man picked up the box and the book bag and started to leave.

"Wait a minute. We need to find out if these plans are what you say they are. We want you to come with us to Mr. West's video store," Sergeant Collins said.

The man looked mad. Sergeant Collins waited.

"All right," the man said.

"You will have to make your robot come with us," Sergeant Collins said.

Patches began to bark.

"He can come along, too," Sergeant Collins said.

The man and the robot walked down Front Street. Sergeant Collins and the boys walked along with them. Patches ran and barked.

At the video store Mr. West said, "Hello, everyone. What can I do for you?"

"We need your help. The boys found these plans. We want to know what they say," Sergeant Collins said.

Mr. West looked at the papers. "Boys, you have found what we have all been looking for."

"Is that why you were at the fair?" Ricky asked.

"That's right. I have been helping Sergeant Collins," Mr. West said.

"What's in the papers?" Ricky asked.

"These are plans for all kinds of robots and plans for making the robots work," Mr. West said.

"Why would someone want robot plans?" Tom asked.

"They are worth a lot of money," Mr. West said.

"You have been taking plans for a long time. These boys have caught you at last," Sergeant Collins said.

"And you have turned your robot into a robber," Eddie said.

"You are going to have to come with me," Sergeant Collins said to the man.

"Can the robot stay with Mr. West?" Tom asked.

"I don't see why not. Is that all right with you, Mr. West?" Sergeant Collins asked.

"Yes, I would like that," Mr. West said.

Sergeant Collins took the man away.

"Do you know how to make the robot sit down, Mr. West?" Eddie asked.

"Yes, I do. The robot must be tired. He has had a long day," Mr. West said.

The boys laughed.